RAINBOW magic ™

The Weather Fairies

Daisy Meadows

ORCHARD

It is a lovely autumn day in Fairyland.
The Weather Fairies are waiting for
Alabaster, their best friend.
They are going to play their favourite
game, hide-and-seek.

Alabaster is a young unicorn.
He lives with his herd in the
Fairyland Forest.
Alabaster loves to play games with
the Weather Fairies.

The fairies hear a whinny.
"Quick! Hide!" whispers Storm.
Alabaster gallops into the orchard.

"Come out! Come out!" Alabaster calls, stamping his hoof. "Have you heard the news?"

The Weather Fairies peek out from behind the leaves. "What news?" Hayley asks.

"The Fairy King and Queen are in the forest," the unicorn says. "They're picking new unicorns to lead their carriage."
"Wow!" Crystal exclaims. "That's an honour."
"I bet all the unicorns want to pull the carriage," Evie adds.

"Yes, my parents are auditioning," Alabaster
says. "Do you want to watch?"

"Absolutely!" Goldie exclaims.
"The auditions are in the clearing,"
Alabaster says.
"Let's go!" says Storm.

Crystal and Storm fly up ahead, while
the other fairies walk with Alabaster.

The King and Queen are already in
the clearing.

"My mum and dad are over there," Alabaster
says. He points with his horn.

"Ooooh," Pearl whispers. "They're wonderful."

The two unicorns run side by side and leap
into the air.

The King and Queen speak to each pair of unicorns.

Alabaster and the Weather Fairies wait.

The King and Queen talk to each other.
At last, the Queen turns to the crowd.
"Our next lead unicorns will be Quicksilver
and Lady Grey," she announces.
Alabaster gasps. "Those are my parents."

The young unicorns gather around Alabaster.
"You get to live in the palace stables," one
unicorn says.
"You're so lucky," adds another.
Alabaster says nothing.

Once the other unicorns have left,
Alabaster sighs.
"What's the matter?" Hayley asks.
"Nothing," he mumbles.
The fairies look at one another with concern.

"You must want to talk to your parents,"
Abigail says.
"Yeah," Alabaster says, kicking the dirt.
"We should head home," Crystal says. "But
we'll see you tomorrow."

Early the next morning, there is a knock at the Weather Fairies' door.
It is Alabaster's parents.

"Alabaster is missing," Lady Grey says.
"We think he's upset about moving."
"We can't find him in this mist," Quicksilver explains. "Can you help?"

"Yes," the fairies say together.
"He would never go far," Crystal insists. "He knows it isn't safe."
"We know all his hiding places," Evie tells them. "We'll find him."

The Weather Fairies fly over the foggy forest and land in the glen.
Evie swirls her wand, and the mist lifts.
Goldie twirls her wand, and the sun comes out. "That should shed some light on things," she says.

They look in Alabaster's favourite hide-and-seek spots, but they cannot find him.

"Alabaster!" the fairies call. "Come out, come out, wherever you are."

"Look! Behind that tree," Pearl declares.
The fairies peek around the tree and see
their friend.

"Alabaster, we're so glad we found you!"
Crystal says.
"Your parents are worried about you," Goldie
tells him.
"They said you are sad about moving,"
Pearl adds.
"I am," Alabaster sighs. "I'll miss my herd. And
I'll especially miss all of you."

"We'll miss you, too. But we'll still see you,"
Abigail says. "We're best friends."
"Promise?" Alabaster asks.
"Promise," the Weather Fairies reply.

The fairies walk Alabaster back to the herd.
His parents are happy and relieved to see him.

"I'm sorry I ran off," Alabaster says.
"We're glad you are safe," says his father.

The King and Queen join them.
"We hope you will enjoy living at the palace,
Alabaster," says the King.

"I think you will especially like the gardens," adds the Queen. "They are wonderful for hide-and-seek."
"Hide-and-seek?" Alabaster says hopefully. The Queen smiles and nods her head.

The Weather Fairies circle around Alabaster and give him a hug.
"We'll miss you so much," Abigail says.

"Will you visit me soon?" Alabaster asks.
"Of course. We're best friends," Evie says.
"Ready or not, here we come!"